My Butt is SO SILLY!

Dawn McMillan

Illustrated by Ross Kinnaird

Dover Publications
Garden City, New York

My butt is so *silly*!

It's unruly and wild.

I need a new butt!

A butt with **manners**.

A butt that is mild.

My butt's **super** active ...
over the top!
It's got to keep **moving**.
No way it can **STOP**.

My butt wants to dance
when it's supposed to be sleeping.
Swinging and *singing*,
swaying and leaping.

Jumping and **BUMPING**.

Behavior so **bad**.

My butt is ridiculous!
My butt acts like a **fool**.
It causes trouble
when I go to school.

The morning goes well.

Until ...

there's a bad smell in Show and Tell.

The classroom's a **riot**.

The teacher wants quiet.

My butt is a **rascal**,
so hard to restrain!
It likes to **JUMP** puddles
and play in the rain ...

To get my pants **dirty**,
worn out and **tattered**,
leaving my folks feeling
worried and shattered.

A problem indeed! My folks think I need
some **quiet time** to sit down and read.
Or … to watch a TV show for a bit.
My butt might relax if it has to sit.

So ...

My butt starts to slouch, here on the couch.
On fluffy cushions, the cushions that slump.
Cushions just right for a butt that goes

bump.

And on the chair where Dad sits at night.

Yes ...

My butt and Dad's chair fit together just right.

So possibly ...

My butt will *chill*. I think it will.

I think it might settle and stay very still.

But ...

A square butt is **interesting**.
A square butt is **rare**.
A square butt fits perfectly
down the back of a chair.

So here I am with my legs in the **air!**

My mom is laughing.
My dad is, too.
And then they do what they need to do …

Pull!

And luckily ...

My **silly** butt is completely intact.
It's all round again and it still has a **crack**.

It's ready to jump. It's ready to play.

And guess what I've found in our yard today ...

My birthday present! A cool trampoline!
It's the best present I've ever seen.

My butt is so happy. It's great at seat drops.

One, then another, the fun never stops.

Seat drops with half twists, five at a time.

My butt's a natural! Its balance is fine.

Now my butt has ambitions.

My butt is **bold**.

My silly butt is aiming for

About the author

Hi, I'm Dawn McMillan. I'm from Waiomu, a small coastal village on the western side of the Coromandel Peninsula in New Zealand. I live with my husband, Derek, and our cat, Lola. I write some sensible stories and lots of crazy stories! I love creating quirky characters and hope you enjoy reading about them.

About the illustrator

Hi. I'm Ross. I love to draw. When I'm not drawing, or being cross with my computer, I love most things involving the sea and nature. I also work from a little studio in my garden surrounded by birds and trees. I live in Auckland, New Zealand. I hope you like reading this book as much as I enjoyed illustrating it.

Bibliographical Note

This Dover edition, first published in 2022, is an unabridged republication
of the work published as *My Bum is SO CHEEKY!* by Oratia Media Ltd.,
Auckland, New Zealand, in 2022. The text has been Americanized for this edition.

International Standard Book Number

ISBN-13: 978-0-486-84976-8
ISBN-10: 0-486-84976-7

Manufactured in the United States of America
84976702   2022
www.doverpublications.com